THE MAGNIFICENT MOO

THE MAGNIFICENT

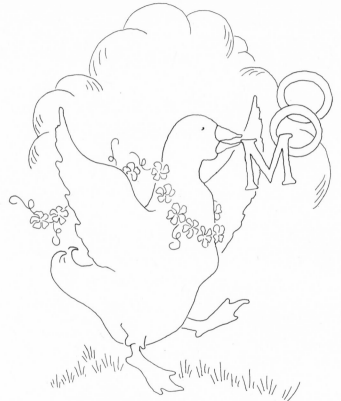

by Victoria Forrester   Atheneum New York 1983

LIBRARY OF CONGRESS CATALOGING IN PUBLICATION DATA

Forrester, Victoria.
  The magnificent moo.

  SUMMARY: When a cow trades her moo for
a cat's meow because she thinks it too loud,
the moo gets traded in turn to several
other animals until it finally returns
to a more satisfied cow.
  [1. Animal sounds—Fiction.   2. Cows—Fiction.
3. Animals—Fiction] I. Title.
PZ7.F772Mag   1983   [E]   82-13781
ISBN 0-689-30954-6

Published simultaneously in Canada by
McClelland & Stewart, Ltd.
Composition by Dix Type Inc., Syracuse, New York
Typography by Mary Ahern
First Edition

For a day in summer
For my son, with love

Once upon a time there was a cow who had a very good life, except for one thing: she was afraid of her own moo.

Every time she opened her mouth to say moo, the sound was
SO BIG
and
SO LOUD
that it frightened her all to pieces.

One morning, the cow was out in the pasture eating grass and little yellow daisies and listening to the gentle sound of the bees, when along came Cat with his usual good morning meow.

"Moo!" said the cow. But she had no more than opened her mouth when out came a sound SO BIG and SO LOUD that there she was again, quite all to pieces.

The cat always felt sorry for the cow when this happened.

"If only you could hear the way your moo sounds to my ears," he told her. "Why yours is a sound as soft and as smooth as sweet butter.

"My meow is a little sound, hardly worth making, but yours is a wonderful sound, a marvelous sound, a truly magnificent moo."

The cat had said the very same thing to the cow many times before; but this morning, as the young cat talked, the cow noticed that his whiskers twitched.

He puffed out his chest, and the cow could tell how much he wished (oh, how he wished!) that he too could make such a magnificent sound.

And so it was that on this particular morning, the cow got an idea she'd never had before.

"Cat," she said, "if you really like my moo so much, how would you like to trade sounds? I would gladly trade my moo for your meow."

And the cat, who'd never had such
a big idea in all his life, said, "Why
yes, I'd be glad to!" Then he thought
for a moment and added wisely, "Only
just for this morning."

So they traded sounds, and the
cow went back to the meadow meowing
happily to herself, while the cat
went on down the road saying, "MOO!"
just as loudly as possible.

Now it wasn't long until the cat
met Duck coming up the road.

"MOO!" said the cat. The duck was so pleased and surprised by what she heard that she fell over backwards and landed right in the middle of a bed of wild nasturtiums.

"Oh, Cat!" said the duck. "What a magnificent moo you have. Where in the world did you get it?

"Thank you," said the cat. "I got it from the cow. We traded sounds with each other, only just for this morning."

"You did?" said the duck. "What a marvelous idea! Could I do it, too? I have a dandy little quack that I would gladly trade for the moo."

And the cat, who, if truth were told, was getting just a bit tired of carrying around such a big moo in his mouth, said, "Yes, I'd be glad to."

So they traded sounds, and the cat went on his way quacking merrily to himself, while the duck went on down the road saying, "MOO!" just as loudly as possible.

Now it wasn't long until the duck met Mouse coming up the road.

"MOO!" said the duck. The mouse was so surprised and delighted by what he heard that he stood straight up on his soft pink toes and sniffed the air in a most excited manner.

"Oh, Duck!" said the mouse in amazement. "What a magnificent moo you have. Where in the world did you get it?"

"Thank you," said the duck. "It's a bit of a story. I got it from the cat, who got it from the cow. We traded sounds with each other, only just for this morning."

"You did?" said the mouse. "What a wonderful idea. Could I do it, too? I have a splendid little squeak that I would gladly trade for the moo."

And the duck, who was getting rather tired indeed of carrying around such a big moo in her bill, said, "Yes, I'd be glad to!"

So they traded sounds, and the duck went back to the pond squeaking softly to herself, while the mouse went on down the road saying, "MOO!" just as loudly as possible.

Now it wasn't long until the mouse met a honeybee buzzing up the road. Busy as usual, she was flying from flower to flower, gathering pollen to make into honey.

"MOO!" said the mouse, and the honeybee was so surprised by what she heard that she did a somersault right in the middle of the air.

"Oh, Mouse!" buzzed the bee with delight. "What a magnificent moo you have. Where in the world did you get it?"

"Thank you," said the mouse. "It's a long story. I got it from the duck, who got it from the cat, who got it from the cow. We all traded sounds with each other."

"You did?" said the bee. "What an amazing idea. Could I do it, too? I have a busy little buzz that I would gladly trade for the moo."

And the little mouse, who was getting very tired indeed from carrying around such a big moo in his mouth, said, "Yes, I'd be glad to!"

So they traded sounds, and the mouse went on down the road saying, "Buzz, buzz, buzz," in a squeaky sort of way, while the honeybee flew quickly from flower to flower saying, "MOO!" just as loudly as possible.

We all know, of course, just how
busy honeybees are, and this bee was
no exception. She was, in fact, so
busy gathering pollen to take to the
hive that she forgot all about
the magnificent moo and flew home
without it. It was left
sitting all by itself right in the
middle of a little yellow daisy.

   Now it just so happened that this
little yellow daisy was growing right
in the same meadow where the cow lived.

So maybe it was the way the moo sounded, coming from the center of a yellow daisy, or maybe it was the way it tickled her ears as it came to her gently on the summer breeze; but whatever it was, when the cow heard the sound, she knew at last that her moo was indeed as soft and as smooth as sweet butter.

So she got right up and looked from flower to flower until she found her moo. And when she found it, she opened her mouth, swallowed hard, and ate it right up, moo and daisy and all.

Then she jumped into the air, clicked her heels, swished her tail, and said, "MOO!" just as loudly as possible. The sound was delicious!

The other animals heard the cow. And once they'd gotten their own sounds straightened out, they all came running to tell the cow how happy they were.

"BUZZ!" said the bee.

"SQUEAK!" said the mouse.

"QUACK!" said the duck.

But the cat said, "PURR!"